REMY AND RUBY'S RESCUE RANCH

HEE-HAW
Help

By Katy Duffield

Illustrated by
Hazel Quintanilla

Rourke
Educational Media
rourkeeducationalmedia.com

A Division of
Carson
Dellosa
Education

Dear Guardian/Educator,
Introduce your child to the wonderful world of reading with our leveled readers. Your growing reader will be continuously engaged as he or she is guided from one level to the next. Each level is carefully built to provide your child with the reading skills and knowledge to be a confident reader! Ultimately, we want your child to develop a love of reading.

Level 1 *Learning to Read*
High frequency words, basic sentences, large type, labels, full color illustrations to help young readers better comprehend the text

Level 2 *Beginning to Read Alone*
Short sentences, familiar words, simple plot, easy-to-read fonts

Level 3 *Reading on Your Own*
Short paragraphs, easy-to-follow plots, vocabulary is increasingly challenging, exciting stories

Level 4 *Proficient Reader*
Chapters, engaging stories, challenging vocabulary, multiple text features

Reading should be a pleasurable experience. A child who enjoys reading reads more, and a child who reads more becomes a better reader. Your child will grow with exposure to broad vocabulary and literary techniques, and will develop deeper critical thinking and comprehension skills. We are excited to be a part of your child's reading journey.

Happy reading,
Rourke Educational Media

Edited by: Kim Thompson
Cover layout and interior layout by: Kathy Walsh
Cover and interior illustrations by: Hazel Quintanilla

Library of Congress PCN Data

Hee-Haw Help / Katy Duffield
(Remy and Ruby's Rescue Ranch)
ISBN 978-1-73161-492-6 (hard cover)(alk. paper)
ISBN 978-1-73161-299-1 (soft cover)
ISBN 978-1-73161-597-8 (e-Book)
ISBN 978-1-73161-702-6 (ePub)
Library of Congress Control Number: 2019932399

Printed in the United States of America,
North Mankato, Minnesota

Table of Contents

Chapter One
New Guy

Remy and Ruby hop down the bus steps. They race to the barn. They can't wait to see the ranch's new **arrival**.

But before they see it, they HEAR it.

Hee-Haw! Hee-Haw!

Remy covers his ears.

"What is *that*?" Ruby cries.

"It looks like a horse," Remy

says. "But horses don't sound

like that!"

"Meet our new donkey, Zora," Auntie Red says.

Chapter Two
Loud Mouth

Zora is a small donkey. But Zora has a BIG voice.

"He has a loud bray for a little guy," Auntie Red says.

"Bray?" Remy asks.

"That's a word for the sound a donkey makes," Auntie Red says.

Auntie Red rubs behind
Zora's floppy ears.

"Is Zora a boy donkey?"
Remy asks.

"Yes," Auntie Red says. "He
is a jack. That is what boy
donkeys are called."

Remy and Ruby climb on the fence. Ruby pats Zora's nose. Remy scratches his back.

"Hey!" Ruby says. "I think he likes us!"

Remy nods. "He is quiet now!"

But the quiet doesn't

last long.

Hee-Haw! Hee-Haw!

The kids jump off the fence.

The chickens **scatter**. The

barn cat screeches.

MEE-OWWW!

Even Auntie Red takes a

step back and covers her ears.

HEE-HAW! HEE-HAW!

"Maybe he is thirsty," Ruby says.

Remy fills the bucket. Zora drinks.

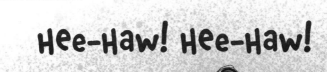

Hee-Haw! Hee-Haw!

"Maybe he is hungry,"

Remy says.

Ruby gets Zora some hay.

Zora eats.

Finally, Zora is quiet.

"Time for **chores**," Auntie
Red says.

Remy and Ruby start to leave. But Zora is not happy about that!

Hee-Haw! Hee-Haw!

Chapter Three
Thanks, Zora!

That night, Remy and

Ruby check on Zora. Auntie

Red rubs behind his ears.

Remy gets him some water.

Ruby feeds him a carrot.

"Maybe that will keep him quiet," Remy says.

"Maybe," Ruby says.

But just as Remy and Ruby

crawl into their beds...

Hee-Haw! Hee-Haw!

Zora's bray is not just loud. It

is the loudest EVER!

"Maybe he is sick," Ruby

says.

"Or lonely," Remy adds.

"We should check on him,"

Auntie Red says.

Auntie Red turns on the porch lights. Something runs into the woods behind the barn.

"What was that?" Remy cries.

"It was a big **coyote**!" Ruby says.

Auntie Red and the kids run

toward the **henhouse**.

They make sure the hens

are okay.

"Donkeys do not like

coyotes," Auntie Red tells them.

"So, he brayed to scare it

away?" Remy asks.

"He did!" Auntie Red says.

"Thanks to Zora, the hens are safe!" Remy says.

"Maybe his bray is not so bad after all," Ruby says.

And Zora has something

to say about that...

Hee-Haw! Hee-Haw!

Bonus Stuff!

Glossary

arrival (uh-RYE-vuhl): Someone or something that has gotten to a place.

chores (chorz): Jobs that need to be done regularly.

coyote (kye-OH-tee): An animal that looks like a small wolf.

henhouse (HEN-hous): A building where female birds raised for their eggs live.

scatter (SKAT-ur): To move off in different directions.

Discussion Questions

1. Why do you think Remy says Zora looks like a horse when he first sees the donkey?

2. What does Zora do when Ruby and Remy start to leave? Why might the donkey have reacted this way?

3. At the end, why do you think Ruby says, "Maybe his bray isn't so bad after all?"

Animal Facts: Donkeys

1. A female donkey is called a jenny.
2. Donkeys often live in groups called herds.
3. Donkeys eat mostly grass and hay.
4. Donkeys can carry heavy loads on their backs.
5. Donkeys like to play with balls and empty cardboard boxes!
6. Donkeys are related to horses and zebras.
7. A donkey's large ears help keep it cool in hot weather.
8. Donkeys love to roll on the ground.

Creativity Corner

What is the loudest sound you've ever heard? How did the sound make you feel? Write a song about the sound and the emotions it made you feel. You can sing it to the tune of your favorite song. Or you can make up your own tune!

About the Author

Katy Duffield is a writer who lives in Arkansas. Loud noises sometimes make her cover her ears, but she thinks she'd like to have a donkey anyway!

About the Illustrator

Hazel Quintanilla loves her job, pajamas, burgers, sketch books, fluffy socks, and of course animals! Hazel had a ton of fun illustrating *Remy and Ruby's Rescue Ranch*.